The Snow Family's Special
Christmas

Written by Stella Gurney
Illustrated by Andrea Petrlik

parfait press

IT WAS CHRISTMAS EVE,

and snow had been falling all day.

The children of Holly Farm were playing outside,

laughing and throwing snowballs at each other.

"Let's build a snow family!" cried the little one.

So they did!

"Mine's Mother!" said the eldest girl.

"Mine's Daddy!" said her sister.

"And mine's the baby!" squealed their little brother.

"Children!" called their mother.
"Come and help me decorate
the Christmas tree."
With a last look at their snow family,
the children ran inside to the warmth.
Out in the cold and gathering dusk,
Mother Snow, Father Snow, and Baby Snow
looked at the warm, golden light pouring
from the windows of the farmhouse.
Inside, they could see the gifts and
decorations glistening on
the Christmas tree.

"I wish WE had a tree to decorate," said Baby Snow.

"Why don't we
sing some carols?"
suggested Mother Snow.

"Jingle bells, jingle bells..."

began Father Snow in an impressive baritone.

"...jingle all the way..."

Mother and Baby joined in.

But halfway through the song, the back door of the farmhouse opened and the farmer looked out cautiously.

"Hello?" he called.

The snow family froze—they could not let the farmer and his family know that they were real.

Through the farmhouse windows
they could see the children hanging
up their stockings by the fireplace
before they went up to bed.
One by one, the lights in the farmhouse went out and the
snow family was left in the silvery light of the full moon.

Baby Snow sighed wistfully.

"I have an idea!" exclaimed Mother Snow.

"Why don't we have our own Christmas?"

"Ooh, yes!" squealed Baby Snow excitedly.

First they decorated a little fir tree

that stood in a corner of the garden.

Father Snow found some icicles hanging from the roof

of the garden shed. He hung them on the branches of the

tree, where they sparkled in the moonlight.

Mother Snow gathered holly and mistletoe berries from

the bushes and scattered them among the branches,

and Baby Snow made snow decorations and

placed them gently around the tree.

Then they laid the garden
table for their Christmas
feast. Father Snow took
three little handkerchiefs
off the clothesline to use
as napkins, Mother Snow
found some small flowerpots
to use as cups,

and Baby Snow
scoured the ground
for twigs to use
as knives and forks.
They stood back to
survey their work.
"Beautiful!"
said Mother Snow.

"I wish we could have a fireplace

to hang stockings, like the children do," said Baby.

"Of course we can!" exclaimed Father Snow.

"We'll build one!"

And when they had made themselves their very

own snow chimney, they hung three stockings taken

from the clothesline on their snow mantle.

Over the fields in the distance, the church

bells chimed midnight. It was Christmas Day!

"*Merry Christmas!*"

said Baby Snow.

"*Merry Christmas, everyone!*"

whispered Mother Snow.

"Why don't we get some sleep?" suggested Father Snow.

"In the morning, we can watch the children in the farmhouse

unwrapping their presents. Won't that be fun?"

Baby Snow smiled a little sadly and nodded.

They all closed their eyes and went to sleep.

Sound asleep,
none of the snow family heard
the soft tinkle of bells coming
down from the sky . . .
nor did they see a pair of
black boots appearing
on their snow chimney.

But perhaps the clop of the reindeer hooves

dancing away through the air woke them . . . because

all at once, they opened their eyes

to see a wonderful . . . Christmas . . . SURPRISE!

In front of them lay a magical snow scene.

The table was laden with snow food, iced drinks,

and wonderful ice sculptures. Their stockings

were bulging with real gifts and the little fir tree

sparkled all over with little twinkling stars.

"It's a snow Christmas!" gasped Mother Snow.

"It's beautiful!" said Baby Snow.

"Let's celebrate!" cried Father Snow.

So they did...

. . . right up until Christmas morning dawned,

when they did not mind becoming snow people again,

for they had enjoyed their very own special Christmas.

The End